Four
Clues
for
Rani

Four Clues for Rani

WRITTEN BY
CATHERINE DALY

ILLUSTRATED BY
JUDITH HOLMES CLARKE,
ADRIENNE BROWN, MERRY CLINGEN,
LOREN CONTRERAS & JILLIAN CLARK

RANDOM HOUSE 🏠 NEW YORK

Library of Congress Cataloging-in-Publication Data

Daly, Catherine.

Four clues for Rani / written by Catherine Daly ; illustrated by Judith
Holmes Clarke ... [et al.]. — 1st ed.

p. cm. — (Disney fairies)

Summary: When Queen Clarion hosts a Fairy Treasure Hunt, Rani is
worried that being partnered with Ronan, the slowest sparrow man in
Never Land, will cause her to lose a bet with Vidia.

ISBN 978-0-7364-2659-6 (pbk.)

[1. Fairies—Fiction. 2. Treasure hunt (Game)—Fiction. 3. Competition
(Psychology)—Fiction.] I. Clarke, Judith, ill. II. Title.

PZ7.D16945Fou 2011

[Fic]—dc22   2010017584

www.randomhouse.com/kids

Printed in the United States of America

10 9 8 7 6 5 4 3 2 1

All About Fairies

IF YOU HEAD toward the second star on your right and fly straight on till morning, you'll come to Never Land, a magical island where mermaids play and children never grow up.

When you arrive, you might hear something like the tinkling of little bells. Follow that sound and you'll find Pixie Hollow, the secret heart of Never Land.

A great old maple tree grows in Pixie

Hollow, and in it live hundreds of fairies and sparrow men. Some of them can do water magic, others can fly like the wind, and still others can speak to animals. You see, Pixie Hollow is the Never fairies' kingdom, and each fairy who lives there has a special, extraordinary talent.

Not far from the Home Tree, nestled in the branches of a hawthorn, is Mother Dove, the most magical creature of all. She sits on her egg, watching over the fairies, who in turn watch over her. For as long as Mother Dove's egg stays well and whole, no one in Never Land will ever grow old.

Once, Mother Dove's egg *was* broken. But we are not telling the story of the egg here. Now it is time for Rani's tale. . . .

Four
Clues
for
Rani

"Oh, cockleshells!" The cry startled a black-capped chickadee. The bird burst out of the brush and into the air right in front of Rani. She gave a little cry of her own.

What in Never Land is going on? thought Rani. She stepped forward and parted a tall clump of Nevergrass. And there, next to Havendish Stream, she saw her fellow water-talent fairy Silvermist.

Silvermist was staring into the water. Her hands were on her hips and she had an annoyed look on her face. Tally, another water talent, was at her side.

"Is everything okay?" asked Rani.

Silvermist looked up. Her long, black hair rippled down on either side of her heart-shaped face. "Oh, Rani. What a disaster! It all started when Tally and I came here to check the stream's water level," she began to explain.

Rani nodded. There had been a dry spell in Pixie Hollow for the past two weeks. Havendish Stream had slowed to a trickle. The stream powered the fairy-dust mill, which was where the fairies kept their grains. They also made fairy dust there.

Each and every water talent had been working round the clock to keep the stream at its usual level. They pulled raindrops out of clouds. They changed the path of underground streams to meet up with Havendish.

The water talents had worked especially hard, but many of the other fairies had helped out as well. Every fairy who needed water for work—the cooking, dyeing, garden, wing-washing, and dish-washing talents, to name a few—had felt the dry spell's impact. It had been a busy two weeks. Exhausting, in fact.

"Luckily, the rains came last night," Silvermist went on. "It looks like—"

"—everything is back in order," Rani finished for her.

Silvermist nodded and returned to the current problem. "So here I was, checking out the water level. Then the clasp of my mother-of-pearl belt came loose and it fell into the stream!"

Rani looked into the water. The belt winked in the sunlight. It seemed right at home in the golden sand at the bottom of the stream.

Tally leaned forward and took a closer look over Silvermist's shoulder. "*Your* mother-of-pearl belt?" she cried. "That's *my* mother-of-pearl belt!"

Silvermist's glow, like every fairy's, was generally lemon yellow with a hint of gold. Suddenly, it became bright orange with embarrassment. "I'd fly backward if I could," she said to Tally, uttering the usual fairy apology. "I meant to return it right away, but it's so pretty, and I thought I'd wear it one more time. . . ." Her voice trailed off.

The water was too deep to reach the belt with a stick. And Silvermist and Tally couldn't go into the stream. Never fairies, even water-talent ones, can't get their wings too wet. When wings get waterlogged, they can drag a fairy under-water. So although Silvermist was des-perate to get the belt back for her friend, going in after it was out of the question. Tally, on the other hand, looked as if she wouldn't mind, at that moment, giving Silvermist a quick shove into the water.

But Rani wasn't like other fairies. Without saying a word, she dove into the stream so cleanly, she hardly made a splash.

Silvermist gasped, but Tally just laughed. "That's right!" she said. "I keep forgetting!"

Rani, you see, had no wings to drag her under. By nature a very generous fairy, she was also rather impulsive. Not so long ago, she had, without a second thought, cut off her wings to help save Never Land from certain destruction.

It was terrible to be without wings, but it did have one advantage. Rani was the only fairy in all of Pixie Hollow who could safely swim.

Rani opened her eyes underwater

and saw the belt right away. Still, she waited before picking it up. She playfully chased a little minnow. She sifted some pale sand between her fingers. She moved her head from side to side and watched her golden hair float around her like a shaft of sunlight.

Only when it felt as if her lungs were going to burst did she reach down and grab the belt. She kicked her legs until her head broke the surface of the stream. She held up the belt.

Silvermist and Tally both reached for the belt at the same time. Tally raised an eyebrow at Silvermist. Silvermist pulled her hand back.

"What would we do without you?" Silvermist said to Rani.

As Tally took her belt, Silvermist helped Rani out of the water. Rani shook herself off. The water sprayed her two friends a bit. Then she sat down on a warm rock to dry off in the sun.

"I didn't mean to get mad at you, Silvermist," said Tally. She hooked the shiny belt around her narrow waist. "I know you didn't drop the belt on purpose. It's just that we've all been on edge these past two weeks. . . ."

Silvermist and Rani nodded in sympathy.

"I even saw two sparrow men get into a shoving match last night. It was over the last mushroom turnover!" Silvermist said, her eyes wide.

"That's terrible!" said Tally. She

thought for a moment, then smiled slyly.
"Those turnovers are delicious, though."

Rani giggled. A baby newt had crept
onto the warm rock with her. It was now
sitting in her lap.

"I overheard Queen Clarion talking to Cinda," said Silvermist. Cinda was one of the queen's helper fairies. "The queen thinks we've all been working too hard. We need a break."

Rani smiled. Queen Clarion was a very special ruler. She was kind and fair, and appreciated every single fairy in her kingdom. From the aphid-wrangling talents to the scrap-metal-sorting fairies, the queen felt they were all equally important.

Silvermist brushed her hands together. "Well, we'd better get back—"

"—to the Home Tree?" Rani finished for her. It was usually hard for Rani to wait for her fellow fairies to finish speaking. She liked to help them along.

Most fairies found this habit terribly annoying, but they were too polite to say so.

"Yes, are you ready to go, too?" asked Tally. "Is Brother Dove on his way?" After Rani had given up her wings, she had been given a new pair in their place—the wings of Brother Dove. Whenever she whistled, he appeared. He took her anywhere she needed to go.

"I think I might stay and practice some water tricks," said Rani. There had been days and days of hard work during the dry spell, and her fingers were positively itching for a little water play.

"That's a nice idea," said Silvermist. "Now that things are normal again, we can finally get back—"

"—to the things we enjoy," Rani said. All three fairies sighed.

"I can't remember the last time I played seashell tiddlywinks," said Tally. The game was a favorite among the water talents.

"Or tic-tac-toad," added Silvermist. Rani was a big fan of seashell tiddlywinks, but tic-tac-toad wasn't for her. Too . . . warty.

Tally bit her lip. "Are you sure you'll be okay?" she asked. "Are you certain Brother Dove will come get you?"

Rani stared at Tally, who went on despite the fact that Silvermist was frowning and shaking her head. "It must be so hard to have to rely on someone else to—"

"I guess we'll see you later, Rani," Silvermist interrupted. She gave Tally a look that meant *Stop talking—now!* With a quick wave, the two fairies took off into the air.

Rani watched them. She felt just a tiny bit wistful as the sunlight glinted off their wings. *It isn't so bad relying on Brother Dove,* she thought. It was the closest thing to having her own set of wings.

She closed her eyes. She had helped save Never Land by making an important decision. Was it hard being the only fairy without wings? Sometimes. But it was also special. She could go to a place no other fairy could visit. A place with fish and seaweed, currents, mermaids, and coral of every color. Most times Rani thought she had made a fair trade. A good one, in fact.

Soon she was no longer soaking wet, just dampish. She gently nudged the still-sleeping newt from her side and began to do some water tricks. First she bounced a water ball around a bit. She stretched it into an oval. Then she molded it into a tricky heart shape.

Next, she made several fountains of various shapes and sizes. Finally, she worked on her water snake. Although it was good enough to scare away the shy little newt, Rani was still not satisfied.

A rumbling in her belly told her that it was almost dinnertime. She had been doing water tricks longer than she'd thought. She whistled for Brother Dove, who flew up almost right away.

"To the Home Tree, Brother Dove," she told him. She settled herself onto the bird's broad back, and they took off into the air.

2

BROTHER DOVE LANDED in the courtyard beside the Home Tree. Rani gave him a pat on the wing as she climbed off his back. But her mind was already thinking about dinner.

She hoped dandelion greens with raspberry dressing would be on the menu. But lately there had been a lot of cream of asparagus soup. She wrinkled her nose. That dish had been served three days in a row already!

Rani walked up the front steps and entered the gleaming entryway of the Home Tree. She was so busy thinking about food that she wasn't paying much attention. She didn't notice the hard-at-work entryway-polishing sparrow man until it was too late.

Her feet slipped right out from under her. "Sweet raindrops!" she cried as she tumbled to the floor.

Rani opened her eyes and found herself looking into the brown eyes of a sparrow man named Ronan. Ronan was one of the slowest and most deliberate fairies in Pixie Hollow. It took him twice as long to do his job as any of his fellow talents.

Most fairies liked him, though. He was laid-back, they said. Some even thought he polished three times as well as the others. But Rani wasn't fully convinced. She'd rather have something

done in a wingbeat. Sometimes she wondered if he wasn't just plain lazy.

"Are you hurt?" Ronan asked. When Rani shook her head, Ronan put out his hand to pull her to her feet.

"I'd fly backward if I could," he drawled. He thought for a moment and grinned. "I certainly didn't mean to send you on a trip!"

Rani gave him a wry smile. *My, he's a slow talker, too,* she thought.

"I was just—" he began.

"—working late?" Rani finished for him.

He shook his head. "No, I was—"

"—taking your time?" Rani offered.

Ronan cocked his head. "No, I mean I was—"

"—daydreaming?" Rani suggested. She was certain she was right this time.

Ronan shook his head again. He had an amused look on his face. "No," he said. "I was just thinking about you, and you came along. What a coincidence!"

"Yes, a coincidence," echoed Rani. She was a little curious about what he'd been thinking. But at the rate he spoke, she might be there all night! She turned to leave. At that moment, Ronan's polishing cloth slipped out of his pocket and fell to the ground.

Quick as a wink, Rani bent to grab it. Ronan leaned forward to pick it up as well. *Clonk!* Their heads bumped— hard. Tears sprang to Rani's eyes. That smarted!

"Oh, dear," said Ronan. A look of concern filled his face. "That was awkward! Are you okay?"

Rani's head ached. She was dreadfully hungry. She wanted to get out of there before Ronan did something like stomp on her foot.

"I'd better go," she replied. "I want to wash up before dinner."

"What's the rush?" asked Ronan, his eyes twinkling. "Think they're going to run out of asparagus soup?"

Rani's stomach replied with a loud rumble. Her glow turned a deep and sudden orange.

Ronan laughed, which only added to Rani's embarrassment.

"I'll see you at dinner, Ronan," she

said. It wasn't easy to be dignified with a growling belly! She began to climb the spiral stairway to the second floor.

"It was a pleasure running into you!" Ronan called. He laughed as he slowly returned to his work. But then a serious look came on his face. "Before you go, I just wanted to say that I understand how hard it must be to—"

Rani paused, her hand resting on the banister. She frowned. She'd had enough sympathy today. Not Ronan, too! "—be the only fairy without wings?" she said. "I'll have you know that it isn't so hard at all." She didn't turn around again.

Rani walked peevishly down the hallway that led to her room. *What a rude sparrow man!* she thought. *Luckily, he's not a water talent, or I would have to talk to him every day!*

Then her thoughts turned to other, more important subjects. *I hope we're not really having asparagus soup again!*

3

RANI KICKED OFF her slippers as soon as she entered her bedroom. She almost always went barefoot in her room. She loved the feel of the river stones that paved the floor. In fact, the whole room was just perfect for her. The driftwood bed and the coral in the corner where she hung her clothes. The blue-green walls.

The woven seaweed curtains and matching quilt. A sprinkling of sand on the floor, some special shells, and a sea-glass mobile were her favorite touches.

Rani filled her washbowl and cleaned her face and hands. Running a comb through her long, blond hair, she looked at her reflection in the water. Her blue eyes were the same color as the deepest of oceans.

Feeling refreshed, she left her room and went downstairs. Snippets of conversation reached her ears as fairies flew by on their way to the tearoom. "She said she's at her wits' end. . . ." "I've been as busy as a nursing talent during an outbreak of fairy pox. . . ." "The water talents are getting all the sympathy,

but who ever thinks about the bread-buttering talents?"

At the tearoom door, Rani stood behind a group of fairies waiting to get in. Ahead of her, an art-talent fairy named Quill said, "Did you hear? Mixie's cake fell because Spinner was doing jumping jacks in the hallway. She stormed out of the kitchen and dumped a bowl of cream filling on his head!"

"Oh, my goodness!" said her companion.

"Yes," Quill said. "And I heard that he made her even angrier by saying, 'How sweet of you, Mixie. Cream filling is my favorite!'"

A smile crept onto Rani's face. That *was* kind of funny. But it was clear that the last two weeks had taken a toll on everyone. It wasn't just the water talents who were worn out—all of Pixie Hollow was on edge. The fairies had been working too hard.

Rani took her spot at the water-talent table. When the serving-talent fairy placed a big bowl of cream of asparagus soup in front of her, Rani must have made a face.

The serving talent whispered, "I know! It's all because of the dry spell!" Thankfully, there were also dandelion green salads and mushroom stew, so Rani ended up enjoying her meal.

As soon as the dinner plates were cleared, one of the queen's helpers tapped a spoon on a goblet made of the

finest fairy crystal. *Cling—cling—cling!*
Queen Clarion was about to make an
announcement.

"Good evening, fairies," the queen
began. Rani had always thought that
Queen Clarion's voice was as lovely as
she was. It sounded like little bells.

"As you are aware," the queen said,
"the recent dry spell has caused us all to
work very hard the past couple of weeks.
I know many fairies are tired and
grumpy."

Rani looked around. Several fairies,
Mixie included, lowered their heads
sheepishly.

"Now Havendish Stream is back to
normal. It's time for a well-deserved
break." The queen paused for a moment

and smiled broadly. "There will be no work tomorrow!"

"Oooh!" The fairies all looked at each other. No work? What would they do all day?

"Instead," the queen went on, "there will be"—she paused for dramatic effect—"a Fairy Treasure Hunt!"

The room started to buzz. The fairies at the water-talent table began chattering. Humidia grabbed Rani's arm. "How exciting!" she cried, her face glowing.

Rani agreed. She couldn't even remember the last time there had been a treasure hunt!

"What's a Fairy Treasure Hunt?" Prilla called over the hubbub.

Prilla, the one and only mainland-visiting-clapping-talent fairy, was a newer arrival. She had not yet taken part in this special event.

"It's a series of fun and challenging clues for you to solve that take you all over Never Land," the queen explained. "You get to pair up with anyone you want."

"And don't forget about the box lunches!" cried a sparrow man. "They're delicious!"

Everyone laughed. The box lunches were a special treat. Each fairy and sparrow man got his or her favorite sandwich, on his or her favorite bread. They picked their favorite cookies, a piece of fruit, and a canteen full of their favorite drink. Rani smiled just thinking of it. She'd have raspberry lemonade for sure.

"How many clues are there?" Prilla wanted to know.

"There are four clues in all," the queen answered. "Tomorrow morning in the courtyard you will pick your partner. Once everyone is paired up, we will hand out the very first clue. If you get it right, it will lead you to the second clue. And so on."

"What is the treasure this year?" asked Vidia in her usual haughty tone. "A shiny silver bauble? A sparkly trinket?" She sounded uninterested, but Rani was close enough to see the gleam of competition in her eye.

"A private luncheon in my gazebo,"

said Queen Clarion. "And afterward, a special viewing of the Fairy Jewels."

There was a gasp. The Fairy Jewels! What a treat! Vidia tried to look indifferent, but Rani knew that even she would be honored to have a private viewing of the special gems and precious objects that had been passed down from fairy queen to fairy queen.

"So come to the courtyard at sunrise," the queen finished. "We will hand out lunches and the first clue to each team." She paused. "May the best fairy team win!"

"Hooray!" the fairies all cheered. Queen Clarion looked pleased. She was a wise ruler who knew how to keep things running smoothly. A day of good-natured competition, of no work, of roaming around Never Land with a friend, was just what the fairies needed. And then things could return to normal.

The serving talents had begun to pass out dessert. Lympia, a laundry-talent fairy, leaned over from her seat at the next table. "Are you as excited about the Fairy Treasure Hunt as I am?" she asked Rani.

"Yes," said Rani. She tried to decide between an acorn tart and blueberry crumble. Maybe the acorn tart today. She reached for it.

Lympia's eyes were sparkling. "You know," she confided, "it's not the clues, or the competition, or even the possibility of winning that I love the best. I spend so much time in the laundry room, it's a treat for me to get to fly all over Never Land. The wind in my wings, the . . ." Suddenly, she trailed off and bit her lip. Rani was confused for a moment. Why was there a flicker of pity in Lympia's eyes?

Then Rani realized what Lympia was thinking. "Yes, I enjoy the view from Brother Dove's back, too," Rani said lightly. She put the dessert back down. She had lost her appetite.

"Oh, it's almost the same thing, isn't it?" said Lympia. But the look on her face told Rani that she didn't believe it, even for an instant.

Now Rani was determined not just to do well in the treasure hunt. She had to win it. She wanted to prove that you didn't need wings to be the best fairy. To prepare, she decided she'd go to the library to look at some maps of Never Land.

The library was empty except for one scribe talent named Tome, who was reshelving some gardening books. Rani gave him a smile, then went straight to work. She pulled books off the shelves and maps off the rack. The words and pictures filled her mind with fairy history, legends, and landmarks.

She learned more than she'd ever thought she'd want to know about fairy-Tiffen relations. She read about Kyto the dragon's ancestors. And she found out that the traditional fairy greeting "Fly

with you" had evolved from the much
wordier "I would happily fly with you to
the farthest reaches of Never Arbor and
to the top of Torth Mountain if you
asked."

What a mouthful!

Tome whispered good night and shut
off all but one of the firefly lanterns.

Rani mumbled a reply, but she was caught up in the story of Captain Hook. Finally, the last lightning bug winked out for the night. Rani fell asleep, her cheek pressed against a page about mermaids.

4

Bang! Rani jolted awake as a door in the Home Tree slammed shut. She looked around, bewildered. Where was she? All around her were books and maps. Oh, dear—she had fallen asleep in the library!

Luckily, she hadn't drooled on the pages of the book she had used as a pillow. The scribe talents would have had a thing or two to say about that! As she yawned and stretched, a thought broke through to her sleepy mind. She was late!

Hurrying into the courtyard, Rani took a quick look around. Most of the fairies were already standing in groups of two. She was even later than she'd thought. Rani breathed a sigh of relief when she spotted her best friend, Tinker Bell. Surely Tink had waited for her!

"Partners?" Rani asked. She touched Tink's shoulder. But Tink turned around with a guilty look on her face. Next to Tink stood Prilla, who was obviously her teammate.

"But you weren't here," Tink said. "I thought you already had a partner."

Rani nodded sadly. She made her way through the crowd. Silvermist had partnered up with a pots-and-pans talent named Zuzu. Rani's friend Lily, a garden talent, was deep in conversation with her partner, Violet, a dyeing talent. Fira, a light talent, was whispering with Bess, an art talent. Amaryllis, a butterfly-herding talent, had chosen Aidan, the crown-repair sparrow man.

"I'm sorry, Rani," said Lily when she saw her friend standing by herself. "If I'd known you didn't have a partner . . ." Her voice trailed off.

Rani gave Lily a wan smile. She was very certain that her friends must have figured she already had a partner. But still, she couldn't help feeling a twinge of doubt. *Maybe nobody wants to be my partner because I don't have wings,* she thought.

She stood to the side, all alone, her heart growing heavier and heavier. Everyone was partnered up. Even—and Rani did a double take when she saw this—even crabby Vidia had found a partner. Vidia raised an eyebrow when Rani wandered by.

Dulcie, a baking talent and Vidia's partner, gave Rani an *If I had only known* look. Rani felt a small amount of satisfaction. But it was short-lived, because the truth was that every fairy had someone. Every fairy except Rani.

Rani's eyes filled with tears. She cried even more easily than most water talents. Thankfully, the sewing talents had made sure that all her dresses had several pockets. She needed them to hold her many leafkerchiefs. She pulled one out and blew her nose loudly.

Suddenly, Queen Clarion breezed over to her side. "Rani, how lucky!" she exclaimed. "You need a partner, and I have the perfect one!"

Rani turned, an eager look on her face. The queen smiled and presented Rani's "perfect partner." Rani's heart sank. Before her stood—Ronan.

Was the queen serious? Ronan was too slow to be a good partner. And he felt sorry for Rani for not having wings. He had said so just the evening before. This was *not* going to work!

Rani smiled at Ronan politely. Then she asked for a private word with the queen.

"Is something wrong, Rani?" Queen Clarion asked with a half-smile on her face. To Rani, it looked as if she had a secret.

"I . . . I . . . don't think Ronan is the best partner for me," Rani managed to say.

"There's no one else," the queen explained. She looked into Rani's eyes. "You might be surprised. I believe you and Ronan are better suited than you think."

"But . . . but . . . ," Rani spluttered. Before she could get the words out, the queen had flown to the top of a nearby rock. The crowd noticed and quieted down. The Fairy Treasure Hunt was about to begin!

Now that everyone had chosen their partners, Queen Clarion announced, the first clues would be handed out.

"One last word of advice," said the queen. "Be sure to think twice and work with your partner. This is all about team-work."

Teamwork, thought Rani. All the other fairies were milling about excitedly. Meanwhile, she watched her partner lower himself to the ground. He leaned back against a toadstool and closed his eyes.

Oh, my goodness! Rani thought. *He's going to take a nap!*

Ronan yawned.

Well, I certainly have my work cut out for me, Rani thought.

5

RANI WAS WORRIED. She had whistled for Brother Dove several minutes ago and he still wasn't there. Maybe he had gone to her room instead? Sometimes he met her on the branch outside her window. She decided to check.

On the way, she glanced back and saw that the queen's helpers had started handing out clue envelopes. A crowd of fairies pushed and jostled to get their clue first. Rani's partner still sat on the ground, watching with amusement.

Well, at least he's awake now, Rani thought.

When Rani reached the Home Tree, Vidia was stretched out on the front steps. Rani simply wasn't in the mood to talk to the prickly fairy. She gave Vidia a curt nod.

"Rani, dearest," the fast-flying talent drawled. Vidia always used terms of endearment she didn't mean. "I'm waiting for my too-sweet-for-words partner. She has decided we can't go on the hunt without a dozen freshly baked maple-nut muffins."

Vidia rolled her eyes. "We're certainly an odd pair, aren't we?" she said. "But not quite as mismatched as you and your partner. Did I see him *napping* out there?"

Rani nodded. She hated to agree with Vidia. But this time Vidia was right. She and Ronan were a real mismatch.

"I doubt you two will get any farther than the dairy barn," Vidia mocked. "I hope you don't mind coming in last."

Rani felt her cheeks get warm. She knew she should just keep going. Talking to Vidia would only make her say something stupid. But she couldn't help herself. "Team Rani is going to beat Team Vidia hands down!" she blurted out.

Oh, dear, why did I say that? she thought in alarm.

For a moment, Vidia looked surprised. Then she recovered and laughed. "Would you like to bet on that?" she asked.

"Fine," said Rani. She put her hands into her pockets. She didn't want Vidia to notice that they were trembling.

"All right, then." Vidia's eyes glittered as she spoke. Rani knew that Vidia was imagining all the awful things she could make Rani do. "If Team Rani beats Team Vidia, your wish will be my command for one week. And if Team Vidia beats Team Rani, you'll do what *I* want."

Rani gulped. That sounded horrid! Was she crazy? What were the chances that a wingless fairy would beat the fastest of the fast-flying talents? She opened her mouth to answer, but nothing came out.

Vidia crossed her arms and arched her eyebrows. "Are the stakes too high

for you, Rani dearest? Having second thoughts?"

"No!" Rani managed to say. "I accept!"

Rani turned and ran inside, her stomach in knots. *What have I gotten myself into?* she wondered.

Upstairs, she quickly checked for Brother Dove, but there was no sign of him. With a sigh, she headed back to the courtyard. By then, the sick feeling had begun to pass. Instead, to her surprise, she only felt excitement.

So what if I made a bet I can't win? And so what if I have the worst—no, scratch that, she thought, remembering Vidia—*the second-worst possible partner in all of Pixie Hollow?* It was Fairy

Treasure Hunt Day, for goodness' sake! It was bright and sunny, with a bit of a cool breeze. There were clues to find and puzzles to solve . . . and Rani loved a good challenge.

The courtyard was nearly empty. Envelopes were scattered everywhere. Many of the teams, eager to start the hunt, had hastily torn open the clues. Hardly pausing to read them, the fairies had taken off into the air.

To her relief, Rani spotted Brother Dove right away. But why were Beck and her partner, Jerome, there? Why was Beck checking Brother Dove's wing? And why did Ronan look so concerned?

Beck looked up and saw Rani. The animal talent gave her a reassuring smile.

"Brother Dove hurt his wing last night," Beck said. "I'm going to bandage it for him, but he shouldn't fly for a couple of days. So he has sent for his relative Cousin Dove to take his place until he's better."

All thoughts of the treasure hunt vanished. "Are you sure he's going to be okay?" Rani asked. Her brow wrinkled with concern.

"I'm sure," said Beck. "He just needs a few days to recover."

Rani reached over and patted Brother Dove's good wing. "Get well, Brother Dove," she said. "Don't worry about me. I'll be fine."

Brother Dove nodded in thanks. Just then, there was a loud fluttering of wings and quite a bit of squawking. Everyone looked up to see a smaller version of Brother Dove land beside them.

"This is Cousin Dove," Beck told them. The bird chirped excitedly, and Beck listened, ready to translate. She looked for all the world as if she was trying not to laugh. "Actually, he says he prefers to be called Hawk," she added.

"Hawk?" Ronan said.

"Hawk?" Rani repeated. Cousin Dove was a bit on the scrawny side, if you asked her.

The bird nodded briskly and made cooing noises.

Beck's mouth twitched at the corners. "Yes, Hawk," she said. "Hawk is honored to be your wings today. And he says that if you like him, he can take over for Brother Dove full-time."

Brother Dove gave Hawk a stern glare, and the little bird had the good sense to look embarrassed. Ronan chuckled, and Rani couldn't help laughing herself. Hawk certainly was a cheeky bird!

"Tell Cousin Dove—I mean Hawk—that I am pleased to have him be my wings." Rani left it at that. She gave Brother Dove a quick squeeze around the neck. Meanwhile, Hawk was chirping away as Beck bandaged Brother Dove's hurt wing.

Beck grinned as she said, "Cousin Dove would also like you to know that his eyesight is so sharp he can see a worm from a mile away. He can fly for days without stopping for food or drink, and—" Just then, Brother Dove made a warning sound, and Cousin Dove stopped bragging. "Well, you get the picture," said Beck. This time she really did laugh out loud.

"Tell him we just need him to fly straight and follow our directions," Rani explained. But she was amused by the eager young bird. He obviously wanted to make a good impression.

"Ahem," Beck's partner, Jerome, cut in.

"Oh!" cried Beck. She had completely forgotten about Jerome. He had been waiting patiently for Beck, and now that things were settled with Rani, he was ready to get started. "I guess I had better go! Are you sure everything is okay, Rani?"

Rani nodded. She watched Beck and Jerome take off into the air. Jerome was pointing in one direction. Beck pointed in another.

"One more thing!" Beck shouted to Rani. "Hawk has a terrible fear of—"

"—criticism?" finished Rani.

"No!" said Beck.

"Lightning?" suggested Rani.

"No!" said Beck. She called out something else, but the wind carried her words away. Rani could see Beck and Jerome arguing, midair. Finally, Jerome shrugged. He took off in the direction Beck was pointing.

Oh, well. Rani guessed she and Ronan would find out what Hawk was terrified of, one way or another.

Queen Clarion came over to where Rani, Hawk, and Ronan were standing. "Remember my words," she told them before she flew away. "Work together. You just may be happy that you overslept, Rani."

Not likely, thought Rani. Then she looked at her partner. *And if I were Ronan*, she imagined, *I would be upset that we were getting such a late start because of me.* But Ronan just grinned back at her.

"Ready?" she asked, eager to get going.

"Not yet," said Ronan.

"Ronan, we're already so far behind everyone!" she cried. But Ronan shook his head.

Rani groaned. What was the problem now?

6

Ronan held up the envelope. "Let's figure out the first clue before we take off," he said.

Rani frowned. "I think we should start flying and read the clue on the way," she suggested.

"I think we should take our time now . . . ," Ronan started to say.

Of course you do, thought Rani. *You never do anything quickly!*

"... rather than fly off in the wrong direction and have to begin all over again."

Rani sighed, but nodded. She nearly wanted to scream as Ronan bent over to pick up a twig to use as a letter opener. Slowly, he unsealed the envelope, took out the clue, folded the envelope into quarters, and put it in his pocket. At last he looked at the clue. He cleared his throat.

"'I may be a place for sitting, but I am royally uncomfortable,'" he read. His brow wrinkled. "'Royally uncomfortable'? What does that mean?"

Ronan sat down on a pebble. He put

his hand to his chin, deep in thought.

With another sigh, Rani sank onto a small toadstool next to the sparrow man. *Hmmm. . . .* Rani thought about the chairs in Pixie Hollow. The chair-talent fairies made sure that they were all super-comfortable, so she knew the clue couldn't be about a fairy-made chair.

"Could it be that chair in the library with the loose spring?" Ronan asked slowly. "It poked me in the—Well, let's just say it was pretty uncomfortable!"

Rani frowned. "I don't think that's it," she said. "I think the important clue here is *royally.* You know, like a king or queen."

Ronan nodded. "Could it be one of the chairs in Queen Clarion's chambers?

That would mean it was royal," he said.

"But it doesn't explain the uncomfortable part," said Rani. *Why are we just sitting here when we could be thinking and flying?* she wondered.

"Rani," Ronan said, interrupting her thoughts. "A chair made of stone would be uncomfortable, wouldn't it?"

"Probably," Rani agreed.

"Isn't there a lookout chair made of stone near the lagoon?"

"Yes!" she cried. She jumped to her feet. "And it's called the Throne! That's definitely it!"

Ronan looked very pleased with himself.

"But where is it?" Rani asked. "I've never been there."

Ronan grinned. He knew exactly where it was. "Follow me, Hawk," he told Cousin Dove. Rani climbed onto the bird's back and off they went.

Well, we've gotten such a slow start we're certainly not going to win, Rani thought. *But maybe we still have a chance at beating Vidia. . . .*

Hawk was a smooth and gentle flier. When they got to the Throne, it was obvious that they were one of the last teams to arrive. Most of the fairies (except for the ones who were examining the broken chair in the library, or those trying to make their way into Queen Clarion's quarters to look at her arm-chairs) had already come and gone.

Rani and Ronan landed on the arm

of the chair. Below them was Captain Hook's ship, the *Jolly Roger*. Rani could picture the crusty old pirate himself pacing the deck. He was probably planning his next skirmish with Peter Pan and the Lost Boys!

The clue was written on the chair in Neverberry ink. It was beginning to fade from the many fairy fingers that had already traced the words.

Rani and Ronan read the words, puzzled. The same message was repeated over and over: *Clue #2! Clue #2! Clue #2! Clue #2!*

Ronan and Rani looked at each other blankly.

"I have an idea," Ronan said.

"What is it?" Rani asked eagerly.

"Let's sit here for a moment or two and talk about something completely different! Clear our minds! We're thinking too hard right now."

Another picture filled Rani's mind. She saw herself as Vidia's servant, dusting her petrified dragonfly collection. Rani shivered. There was no time for this—they had to keep moving!

Rani stood up. "Let's head to . . . Second Stone Pass," she said, thinking quickly. "That's a good a guess as any. Let's give it a try."

Ronan shook his head but got up without argument. "After you," he said to Rani.

"Second Stone Pass," Rani said to Hawk. "And hurry!" The little bird took

off with a sudden lurch. Rani threw her
arms around his neck to keep from
falling.

Second Stone Pass was deserted.
After a thorough search, it was clear that
no clue was to be found there.

Rani stamped her foot. Now Vidia was sure to beat her!

"Clue Number Two! Clue Number Two! Clue Number Two!" Ronan started chanting.

Rani turned toward him. "Ronan, I don't see how this is helping," she said.

"Clue Number Two! Clue Number Two! Clue Number Two!" he repeated.

Rani gritted her teeth. She was certain she would scream if he said it one more time.

"Clue Number Two!" he exclaimed.

"Ronan . . . ," Rani said in a warning tone. But then she had a sudden realization. "Say it again!"

"Are you sure?" asked Ronan. "It's not getting on your nerves?"

"No, say it again!" Rani insisted.

"Okay," said Ronan. "Clue Number Two! Clue Number Two! Clue Number Two!"

Rani's eyes widened. "That's it!" she blurted out. "It's an echo!"

"An echo?" asked Ronan.

"Yes, an echo!" Rani cried. "Echo Cavern, to be exact!" She jumped up, ready to go.

"Well, aren't you clever," Ronan said. He gave Rani an admiring look.

Rani smiled, but her grin faded at Ronan's next words. "Now let's pause for a minute and figure out the quickest way to get there," he suggested.

Rani groaned.

7

WHEN A FAIRY HAD a secret she was bursting to tell, she went to Echo Cavern. She shouted the secret into the air. It echoed over and over again until it finally faded away. Once it did, the fairy always felt much better.

Taking a shortcut through Bramble-berry Patch, Ronan and Rani were at

Echo Cavern in no time. "We'll be back soon, Hawk," Rani told the little bird.

Just then, two dairy-talent fairies landed nearby. Rani was pleased as Neverberry punch to discover that she and Ronan had finally caught up to some of the others. *We're not so far behind!* she thought.

Rani and Ronan fell into step and entered the cavern after the two fairies. It was large and sprawling, with passages that led to caves of different shapes and sizes. A fairy could get lost inside for days if she wasn't careful!

Rani pulled a lantern out of her pack. "Good thinking!" said Ronan.

"How will we know which is the right echo?" Rani whispered to him.

"I'm not sure," he replied—rather unhelpfully, Rani thought.

"I lost Bess's favorite paintbrush . . . paintbrush . . . paintbrush . . . ," a voice whispered at the entryway.

Ronan tapped Rani on the shoulder and shook his head. That wasn't the clue.

"I think I'm the prettiest fairy in all of Pixie Hollow . . . Pixie Hollow . . . Pixie Hollow . . . ," the next message echoed.

"Hmph! Everyone knows *I'm* the prettiest," one of the dairy-talent fairies said. Ronan stifled a chuckle.

They came to the end of the passage. The dairy talent and her partner headed one way. Rani and Ronan chose to go to the left.

"I'm jealous of Lily's buttercups . . . buttercups . . . buttercups . . . ," came the next echo. That wasn't it, either.

Ronan and Rani passed several side caves. Without asking each other, they both kept going in the same direction—straight ahead.

Rani practically chortled when she heard Vidia's voice ring out from a cave to their right. "No, precious, I don't want another maple-nut muffin! What I *do* want is to find the next clue!" They were wing to wing with Vidia! Maybe Rani would beat her after all!

Rani and Ronan walked until they came to another part of the cave where the passageway branched off in two directions. Should they go left or right?

Rani raised her lantern and spotted a crack in the wall next to them. Or was it an entrance to a side cave?

Rani leaned forward to take a better look. She stuck her hand out—and it passed deep into the crack. It *was* a cave!

"Should we give it a try?" she asked Ronan. He nodded.

The opening was narrow. It was a tight fit, but Rani slid through. Ronan squeezed through as well.

They found themselves in a tiny stone room. The walls dripped with an eerie glowing moss. Rani looked at Ronan. Were they in the right place?

Then a voice began to speak. This message seemed different from the others. The voice sounded like little bells. It was the queen! "You'll find the next clue deep in the currents . . . currents . . . currents . . . ," her voice said.

Rani and Ronan grinned at each other. What a stroke of luck! They could have wandered around the cavern for hours, but they had stumbled upon the clue right away! They rushed out of the cave, nearly tripping over their feet in their hurry.

Soon they reached the mouth of the cave and stepped outside. They blinked in the sudden sunlight.

Rani grabbed Ronan's arm. "We don't have a moment to lose!" she said. All in a rush, she told Ronan about the bet with Vidia.

He gave a low whistle. "I'm not sure if that's the bravest thing I've ever heard," he said, "or the silliest."

Rani smiled. "A little of both?" she said.

Ronan chuckled. "A little of both," he agreed. "And now I know how high the stakes are. We have to be careful. We don't want to end up in the wrong place again. We need to take things slow."

What? Rani didn't understand Ronan. Shouldn't they speed things up instead?

"Maybe we can take the *next* clue slow," she said. "This one is pretty easy. The voice said 'in the currants.' There's only one place it can mean—Currant Grove!"

Currant Grove was where cherries, cranberries, and currants were grown. "Let's go there before Vidia finds the clue!" She whistled to Hawk and climbed onto his back.

"It could mean *currant*, as in *Currant Grove*," Ronan said slowly, "or it could mean *current*, as in *right now*. Or it could mean—"

Rani gasped. Of course! How had she overlooked that meaning? "Current Pass!" she exclaimed. She slapped her palm against her forehead. "Hawk, to Current Pass, as fast as you can!"

As Hawk took off like a hawk, Rani held on for dear life. Ronan's wings beat double-time to keep up with the eager young bird.

How embarrassing! Rani had confused *current* with *currant*! She could have understood that mistake if she'd been a harvesting or a baking talent, but she was a *water-talent* fairy!

Rani stole a glance at Ronan. He must think she was an idiot! But Ronan only seemed concerned about keeping up with Hawk.

Several fairy pairs flew by Rani and Ronan, clearly coming back from Current Pass. They were on their way to the next clue. But Rani took comfort in this. It meant she and Ronan were headed in the right direction!

Hawk landed rather bumpily on the grass beside the river. Rani climbed off his back and began searching for the next

clue. "Where can it be?" she asked.

Ronan touched her hand. "We'll find it, Rani. We just need to take our time." Rani took a deep breath. She cupped her hand to shield her eyes. And there, in the middle of the water, she could see a message written on a rock that poked above the surface.

"I'll fly out to read it," Ronan offered.

"Nonsense," said Rani. "We'll both go." She hopped onto Hawk's back and they all took off.

But as they were about to read the clue, a piercing scream tore through the air. Ronan and Rani looked up. A hawk was headed straight for them!

With a terrified squawk, Hawk twisted away from the dive-bombing bird. And Rani was suddenly airborne, a fairy without wings, tumbling toward the earth.

8

Splash! Rani fell into the water. The currents at Current Pass, as you would imagine, were strong, but Rani was a good swimmer. She bobbed up to the surface and, to her shock, saw Ronan, about to jump into the water to save her!

"No, Ronan!" she shouted. "I can swim! And," Rani added as she pulled herself onto a big rock, "you can't."

In the excitement, Rani had forgotten about the hawk. But the hawk hadn't forgotten about them. It swooped down for a second time.

Despite her panic, Rani's instincts took over. She dove into the water, narrowly escaping the hawk's sharp claws. In an instant, she came back up. Ronan was flattened against the rock. The hawk kept dive-bombing him.

How could Rani help Ronan? Even animal talents were afraid of hawks. What could a water talent do against such a huge bird?

Suddenly, she remembered one of the water tricks she had practiced. It wasn't perfect yet, but it would do. With

a flick of her hands, a large water snake reared its angry head out of the swirling currents. The hawk swooped down again. Its claws caught Ronan's jacket.

At that moment, Rani used all her powers to make the water snake jump out of the water. The snake lashed its fangs at the hawk. The hawk pulled back, and Ronan wriggled free. The screaming hawk took off, the tattered jacket in its claws.

Rani climbed out of the water and sat on the rock next to Ronan. "You saved my life," Ronan said.

Rani wrung out the hem of her dress, pleased at the compliment. "Not so bad for a fairy without wings," she said.

Ronan looked puzzled. "What do you mean?"

Rani turned away. She couldn't meet Ronan's eyes. "Yesterday in the entryway," she reminded him. "You said that it must be hard to be the only fairy without wings."

Ronan's brow wrinkled as he tried to remember. Then he smiled. "Rani, *you* said that. You finished my sentence for me. I wasn't going to say that at all. I was going to say that it must be hard to be a water talent during a dry spell."

"Oh." Rani's cheeks got warm. "Oh, I see." She paused. "But weren't you disappointed to be paired up with me?"

Ronan looked at Rani as if she had three heads. "Rani," he said, "I thought

I was lucky. You are the bravest, most generous fairy in all of Pixie Hollow. I admire you."

Rani could feel her glow getting very orange indeed. The bravest fairy in all of Pixie Hollow! That was the nicest thing anyone had ever said about her.

"But what about you? Were *you* disappointed?" Ronan asked.

Rani took a deep breath. "At first I was. But you make me stop and think things through. Queen Clarion is right. We *are* a good team."

"Friends?" asked Ronan.

"Good friends," said Rani.

They grinned at each other.

Just then, Rani jumped up. "The clue!" she shouted. She had been sitting right on top of it! "'Unscramble me and you will see,'" she read, "'the name of a well-known tree.'"

"The Home Tree!" Rani cried.

Ronan shook his head. "I don't think so," he said. "*Home Tree* has only eight letters. And this has"—he counted off the letters on the rock—"twelve."

"Oh." Rani sat back down.

Ronan read the letters out loud. "O-R-A-B-I-K-H-Y-E-R-Z-C."

Rani's mind whirled to unscramble the letters. "Oak biz cherry!" she yelled. But neither she nor Ronan had ever heard of a tree with that name.

"Is there such a thing as a yak birch?" Rani asked.

Ronan looked at her blankly for a moment. "No," he said slowly. "But there is the Zebra Hickory. A table in the entryway is carved from one of its branches. And I know where it is, too!"

Rani sprang to her feet. They were back in the game! Once they had made it to land—Rani swimming and Ronan flying—Rani whistled for Hawk. They waited. And waited.

"Um, Rani, I don't think Hawk is coming back," Ronan finally said.

"Oh, dear," she said. "That must be what Beck was trying to tell me. Hawk is terrified of . . . hawks."

The two fairies looked at each other. What were they going to do? Suddenly, Rani's shoulders started shaking. Ronan let out a loud guffaw. They laughed and laughed. After several minutes, their giggles tapered off. Rani felt happier than she had in days.

"I guess we could eat our lunch," she suggested. And that was when they realized that their special box lunches were now at the bottom of Current Pass. For some reason, this made them laugh even harder.

So the two fairies set out for the Zebra Hickory on foot. It didn't matter anymore whether they won or lost. They had solved all the clues so far. They had successfully battled a hawk. And they were a great team, no matter what.

9

"ARE WE THERE yet?" Ronan asked, only half jokingly.

Rani smiled. It was funny for Ronan to be impatient. But then again, most fairies were not used to walking long distances, as she was. She had suggested that Ronan fly to the tree on his own, but he wouldn't hear of it.

"We're a team," he had said. "We'll see this through together, every step of the way."

Ronan was limping by the time they reached the Zebra Hickory. Rani stopped short when she saw the tree. Its wood was striped brown and tan. But even more unusually, Tootles, a Lost Boy, stood by it. He looked thoroughly annoyed.

"It's about time!" he said. "Peter and the rest of the Lost Boys made me stay behind. They're having a huge slingshot battle—without me!"

He reached into his pocket and pulled out a wrinkled clue. He cleared his throat. "'Go straight to the Fairy Circle,'" he read. "'And when you see me, please stand on your head and oink like a pig. Sincerely, Queen Clarion.'"

Normally, Rani would have raced off now and asked questions later. But she had learned a valuable lesson from Ronan. She stopped and thought for a moment, and in that moment, she realized that something wasn't quite right.

"'Oink like a pig'?" she asked. "Queen Clarion wants us to oink like pigs? That's strange."

"Can I see that clue?" Ronan asked Tootles.

The Lost Boy scowled and held the clue high above the fairies' heads so they could take a quick glance. "You see with your eyes and not with your hands," he said. He shoved the clue back into his pocket. But when he bent over to pick up

his slingshot, the clue slipped out of his pocket and fluttered to the ground.

"Bye, fairies," Tootles said. "Good luck with your treasure hunt. Oink, oink!" He ran off.

Once he was gone, Rani and Ronan raced to the fallen clue. They unfolded it and took a close look.

Go strait to the Fairy Circul.
And when you see me pleese stand on
your head and oink like a pig.
    Sinceerly,
    Queen Claryon

Rani shook her head. "Queen Clarion has beautiful handwriting," she said.

"And she also knows how to—" Ronan started.

"—spell," Rani broke in.

Rani looked at the note again. "Especially her own name," she added.

"It's a fake clue!" Ronan exclaimed.

Rani shook her head. That Peter! He was such a trickster, and loved to play practical jokes. He probably hadn't been able to resist pulling a prank on his friend Tinker Bell. And the rest of the fairies got caught in the joke as well.

Now all Rani and Ronan needed was to find the real clue. They looked around in dismay. The ground was littered with pinecones, dead bugs, and rocks. After sorting through piles of leaves, walnut shells, and several mean drawings of

Captain Hook, Rani spotted a piece of paper crumpled into a ball. She smoothed it out. It was the clue! And it was written in the queen's elegant handwriting.

"'You're almost there! Meet me at the Fairy Circle and say "I would happily . . ."'" Rani's voice trailed off.

It was impossible to read the rest of the clue. It had obviously gotten wet. The words were a black, inky blur.

They stared at the clue in dismay. "Let's just head back," Ronan finally said. "At least we'll enjoy the moonlight picnic tonight."

Rani sadly agreed. It was disappointing. They had worked so hard and come so close. But it was time to call it a day.

10

"I WISH WE HAD a balloon carrier," Ronan said for the third time. "Then we could get back in no time."

Rani smiled. "We're not far from Havendish Stream! We'll walk there—slowly," she said, seeing Ronan wince, "make a leaf boat, and sail back. After that, it's just a short walk."

"Good idea." Ronan nodded.

The two headed toward the stream, pausing to eat one blueberry each along the way. It wasn't a famous box lunch, but the berries were sweet and juicy and filled their bellies nicely. Rani laughed at Ronan's blue lips, and he pretended to be upset.

Once at the stream, they picked the strongest, sturdiest leaf. Rani settled herself on it as Ronan pushed them off the bank with their oar, which was made out of a twig. The currents moved them along quickly. On the way, Rani pointed out interesting sights—a school of Never minnows, some extra-huge lily pads, an old bullfrog with the funniest croak, and a dragonfly with purple wings.

They talked about favorite books and songs. They discussed Ronan's talent. Rani was surprised to learn that there were so many different polishing methods—the clockwise stroke, the up-and-down, the back-and-forth—and lots of cloths to choose from.

They talked about Rani's talent and the amazing water snake she had made. They wondered about poor Hawk, who must have been absolutely terrified to have left them like that.

"I hope he's okay," said Rani.

"I hope he hasn't died of embarrassment!" said Ronan.

They imagined the various terrible things that Vidia would make Rani do if she won. "It won't be as bad as all that, will it?" Rani said. After a moment, she added, "You know what? I don't even care anymore! It's only for a week, anyway. Today turned out to be such an adventure, it was worth it."

Soon the little leaf boat bumped against the shore in Pixie Hollow. Ronan flew onto the bank, then reached down and gave Rani a helping hand. The two walked through the woods toward the Fairy Circle.

"For some strange reason I feel nervous," Rani confessed. "Even though I know we're last." The whole time, Rani had been wondering about the note from the Zebra Hickory. What could the rest of the queen's message be? And why did it sound so familiar?

At last, they reached the Fairy Circle. Queen Clarion stood in the center of a group of fairies and sparrow men. A hush fell over the crowd as Pell and Pluck, two harvest talents, flew toward the queen. She smiled. But her face fell when Pell and Pluck flipped onto their heads. "Oink! Oink!" they cried.

There was a moment of silence, then a great roar of laughter. Each and every fairy had done the same thing upon their return. Some had said "Oink, oink," while others had snorted. Some went so far as to imitate the squealing of a pig in danger. Everyone enjoyed watching their fellow fairies repeat their mistake.

For her part, Queen Clarion was fairly certain it hadn't been such a good idea to leave the last clue anyplace where the Lost Boys could get their hands on it. Never in the history of the Fairy Treasure Hunt had there been no winner!

Nervously, Rani and Ronan stepped forward. *If only I could remember the end of that message . . .* , Rani thought.

"Ah, Rani and Ronan," the queen said. "You are the last team. Do you have anything to say to me?" The crowd leaned forward. Smiles twitched at the corners of their mouths. Ronan cleared his throat. Rani took a deep breath.

"'I would happily . . . ,'" they began. The queen's face lit up. But their voices trailed off. Then, suddenly, the words came to Rani, as clear as day. "'. . . fly with you to the farthest reaches of Never

Arbor and to the top of Torth Mountain if you asked,'" she finished, her voice strong and confident. Ronan looked at her, his mouth open in shock.

"I read it last night when I was doing my research," she explained, hardly believing it herself. "And it just came back to me."

The queen's face broke into a wide smile. She turned to address the crowd. "Congratulations to Rani and Ronan—the winners of this year's Fairy Treasure Hunt!"

The crowd gasped. Then cheers erupted. "Hip, hip, hooray!" the fairies shouted.

Queen Clarion clapped her hands with delight. "I knew you could do it! I knew the two of you would make an excellent team!"

Just then, a dove landed nearby. "Hawk!" Rani cried. "I was worried about you!"

The little bird looked dreadfully ashamed.

"Don't feel bad. We're just glad you're okay, Hawk," said Rani.

That night, at the moonlight picnic, Rani and Ronan ate twice as much as any other fairy. Fairy after fairy had asked Rani to sit with them, but she wanted to share the moment with her partner.

"How did you do it?" Tink wanted to know.

Rani smiled at Ronan. "Teamwork," they said together.

"And patience," Rani added. "My partner taught me to take my time and think things through."

Rani and Ronan lay back on their blanket and watched as the light talents put on a show in their honor. Then the music talents sang for them. It was a fantastic evening, one Rani would never forget. But the next day would be wonderful as well. First she and Ronan were having lunch with the queen. Then they were going to see the Fairy Jewels.

"Excuse me, darling." Rani looked up to see Vidia bearing a plate of Rani's favorite dessert—blackberry cupcakes. "Is there anything else I can get for you?" she asked with a sneer.

"A cup of elderflower tea would be

nice," replied Rani. She tried hard not to grin. "With a teaspoonful of clover honey, if you please."

Vidia sighed and turned to go.

"And breakfast in bed tomorrow morning," Rani added with a twinkle in her eye.

"But of course," Vidia said through

gritted teeth. She shook her head and flew away as fast as a fast-flying fairy could go.

Rani and Ronan watched her, then settled back onto their blanket. "Today," said Ronan, "was an amazing day. We saw so many incredible things." He paused. "But *that* is probably the most incredible thing I've ever seen!"

Queen Clarion's Secret

Just as Prilla was about to land, a shadow
crossed the ground in front of her. She looked
up and her eyes widened. A huge bird was soar-
ing across the sky. It was unlike any bird Prilla
had ever seen. The bird was as colorful as a par-
rot, but it was much longer. Its wingspan was as
wide as an eagle's.

The bird traveled so fast that it left a multi-
colored streak in the sky behind it. Prilla felt a
shiver of fear. A bird so big and fast could be
dangerous to fairies. She would have to warn the
queen.

But when she looked back, Queen Clarion
was gone.

Myka Finds Her Way

Myka had to get closer. She had to see what was happening. She flew toward the noise and lights. The rumblings turned to roars. The flashes grew brighter.

Everything looked strange in the on-again, off-again flare of light. *Boom!*

She saw a gnarled tree bent over, its bare branches sweeping the ground. *Boom!* She spotted a towering beehive. It swayed from the thick trunk of a maple tree.

She swerved around it and kept flying. *Boom!* The spooky light cast long shadows from trees . . . plants . . . rocks. Everything seemed different. But she was a scout. She had to keep going.